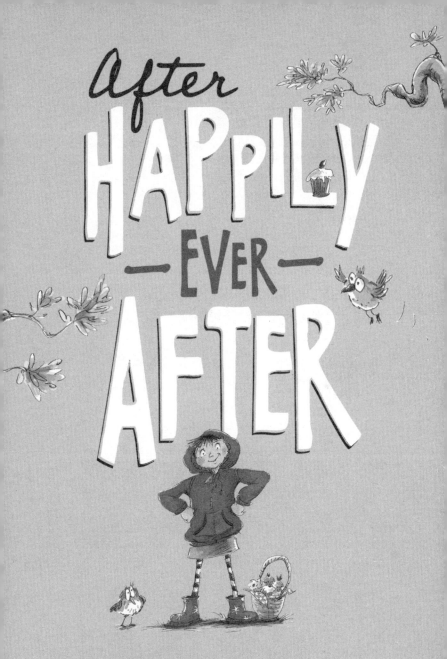

After
HAPPILY
— EVER —
AFTER

Red Riding Hood
Takes Charge

After Happily Ever After is published by Stone Arch Books
A Capstone Imprint
1710 Roe Crest Drive
North Mankato, Minnesota 56003
www.capstonepub.com

First published by Orchard Books, a division of Hachette Children's Books
338 Euston Road, London NW1 3BH, United Kingdom

Library of Congress Cataloging-in-Publication Data is available
on the Library of Congress website.

ISBN-13: 978-1-4342-6413-8 (paperback)

Summary: Little Red Riding Hood is worried about her Granny. Granny's
recovered from her scare with the Big Bad Wolf, but she's lonely. Thankfully
Little Red Riding Hood is on the case! She is ready to find her Granny some
new hobbies and some new friends.

Designer:
Russell Griesmer

Photo Credits:
ShutterStock / Maaike Boot, 5, 6, 7, 52, 53, 54, 55

Printed in China by Nordica.
0114/CA21302400
122013   007937R

After
HAPPILY
— EVER —
AFTER

Red Riding Hood
Takes Charge

by TONY BRADMAN
illustrated by SARAH WARBURTON

STONE ARCH BOOKS®
a capstone imprint

Table of Contents

So Little Red Riding Hood
and her Granny lived
happily ever after.
And then ...

CHAPTER ONE

Little Red Riding Hood headed down the woodland path, a basket of cupcakes in one hand and a bunch of flowers in the other.

It would be her first visit to Granny's for a while, and she hoped everything was okay. After all, it wasn't long since their scary incident with the Big Bad Wolf.

If it hadn't been for that nice man, Mr. Woodcutter, Little Red Riding Hood hated to think what might have happened.

She felt guilty too. Anyone else would probably have realized what the Big Bad Wolf was up to. But she hadn't, and Granny had almost paid a terrible price for her mistake.

Little Red Riding Hood sighed and told herself to be a lot more careful in the future.

"Who's that?" Granny called out when Little Red Riding Hood knocked on the cottage door. "You'll have to show me some ID!"

"It's all right, Granny," said Little Red Riding Hood. "It's me!"

Granny was pleased to see her and gave her a big hug and kiss.

"How are you?" asked Granny. "Is everything okay at school?"

"I'm fine," said Little Red Riding Hood. "But how are you?"

"Oh, I'm all right," said Granny. "Although I have to admit I do sometimes get a bit lonely out here."

"Lonely?" said Little Red Riding Hood.

"Did I say lonely?" laughed Granny. "Don't worry, sweetheart, I'm all right. Mmm, these cupcakes are delicious, aren't they?"

CHAPTER TWO

Later that afternoon, Little Red Riding Hood trudged home, feeling guiltier than ever.

She should have realized Granny was lonely. Granny didn't have any neighbors, and Mom and Little Red Riding Hood lived too far away to visit her often.

"Hello there, Little Red Riding Hood!" a voice roared suddenly. A large, hairy figure appeared beside her.

"Yikes!" she squeaked. "Oh hi, Mr. Woodcutter. Sorry, you startled me."

"No problem," he boomed, smiling at her.
He was a big man with a big beard. He was
about the same age as Granny.

"Just been to see your Granny?" he asked.
"How is she?"

"Well, mostly okay," said Little Red Riding
Hood. Then she told him what Granny
had said.

"A wonderful woman like your Granny feeling lonely?" he said. "I can hardly believe it! I would have thought she'd have plenty of visitors."

"Still, we are rather isolated in this part of the forest. I get lonely myself sometimes. Maybe I could stop over and see her," he added.

"Don't worry, Mr. Woodcutter," said Little
Red Riding Hood. "It's kind of you to offer,
but I'm sure I can think of something.
Anyway, I'd better be getting home now.
Goodbye!"

That evening, Little Red Riding Hood sat in her room feeling bad. She would just have to visit Granny more often. But that might not be easy. There was hardly a day when she didn't do something after school.

CHAPTER THREE

The next day, Little Red Riding Hood thought she could get to Granny's and still be back in time for swimming.

Granny was surprised, but pleased, of course. And she seemed even more pleased when Little Red Riding Hood told her about the woodcutter.

"He asked about me?" said Granny, patting her hair. "Did he really?"

Little Red Riding Hood couldn't stay long. She hurried back, but she was late for swimming.

She went to see Granny the next day, and the next, and the day after.

And she was late for her piano lesson and karate.

And she nearly missed Brownies.

There was another problem too. Little Red Riding Hood was running out of things to talk to Granny about.

"Cheer up, Little Red Riding Hood!" somebody roared. She jumped, but she knew it was only Mr. Woodcutter.

"Why the sad face?" he asked. Little Red Riding Hood explained what was worrying her now.

"I'm sure Granny loves seeing you, whatever you talk about," said the woodcutter.

"Maybe your Granny could do with
company her own age from time to time,
someone she's got more in common with,
someone like . . ."

"You might be right," said Little Red Riding Hood before he could finish what he was going to say. "It's worth a try, anyway! Goodbye!"

CHAPTER FOUR

That evening, Little Red Riding Hood searched The Forest Web and found something that looked promising. She signed Granny up for it.

"The club is called The Forest Belles, Granny," she said on her next visit. "And it's for people just like you — older ladies who live on their own. They meet twice a week and go on great trips. I bet you'll love it!"

But Granny didn't. She hated it and
stopped going after a week.

"I'm sorry, sweetheart," she said, "but being with a bunch of old ladies isn't my cup of tea. I mean, all they did was gossip and complain."

Little Red Riding Hood trudged homeward down the woodland path, even more worried than ever. She bumped into the woodcutter again.

"I see things aren't going well," he boomed.

Little Red Riding Hood explained about The Forest Belles.

"Can't say I blame Granny for feeling that way," said Mr. Woodcutter. "Sounds to me as if she'd prefer the company of one person. I could always . . ."

"I don't know, Mr. Woodcutter," Little Red Riding Hood said gloomily. "It would have to be the right person, but who could that be?"

The woodcutter smiled broadly at her, but she didn't notice.

"You do have a point, though," she said. "Thanks for the advice. Goodbye!"

Mr. Woodcutter's shoulders sagged, and he sadly turned away.

CHAPTER FIVE

That evening, Little Red Riding Hood checked The Forest Web again. She soon found something else that looked promising.

"It's called Forest Speed Dating, Granny," she said on her next visit. "They even have a Senior Citizens Night at the Palace Community Center. You'll meet lots of nice people, maybe even somebody special."

But Granny didn't. She hated it even more
than The Forest Belles.

"I'm sorry, sweetheart," she said, "but I'd rather spend more time with just one person at a time. Then we can get to know each other."

Little Red Riding Hood was filled with gloom. What else could she do?

She trudged home through the forest, and there was Mr. Woodcutter. He asked about Granny, and they chatted for a while. Then he sighed.

"Well, I'd better go," he said. "Oh, I meant to tell you. I'm thinking of moving away to start a new life somewhere else."

"Really? How wonderful!" said Little Red Riding Hood. "Well I ought to be getting home myself. All the best, Mr. Woodcutter. Goodbye!"

She walked down the path, thinking about
Granny. And suddenly the answer hit her.
She had known the right person all along—
Mr. Woodcutter! Why hadn't she seen it
before?

She frowned when she thought of how she ignored him each time he offered to visit Granny.

And now he was planning to move away and take Granny's chance of happiness with him. Little Red Riding Hood decided she wasn't going to ruin things for Granny again!

CHAPTER SIX

So the next day, there was a knock on Mr. Woodcutter's door. He was surprised to see Little Red Riding Hood.

"Hi, Mr. Woodcutter," she said. "I'm on my way to visit Granny, and I wondered if you'd like to come. I'm sure she'd love to see you!"

Mr. Woodcutter smiled. "I thought you'd never ask," he said.

Granny and Mr. Woodcutter got along so
well that within a month, they announced
they were getting married.

It was a wonderful wedding. Little Red
Riding Hood was Granny's bridesmaid.

There was even a picture on the front page of *The Forest Times*.

And Granny and Mr. Woodcutter and Little Red Riding Hood really did live happily ever after!

ABOUT THE AUTHOR

Tony Bradman writes for children
of all ages. He is particularly well
known for his top-selling Dilly the
Dinosaur series. His other titles
include the Happily Ever After
series, The Orchard Book of Heroes
and Villains, and The Orchard
Book of Swords, Sorcerers, and
Superheroes. Tony lives in South
East London.

ABOUT THE ILLUSTRATOR

Sarah Warburton is a rising star
in children's books. She is the
illustrator of the Rumblewick
series, which has been very well
received at an international level.
The series spans across both
picture books and fiction. She has
also illustrated nonfiction titles
and the Happily Ever After series.
She lives in Bristol, England,
with her young baby and
husband.